"PRAISE FOR *THE PUDDLE CLUB*"

"Golf is a journey to discover yourself and your soul. The Puddle Club has it covered under every angle."

—Claude Brousseau PGA Master
- Maui School of Golf

"Jump right into The Puddle Club, the most imaginative introduction to our great game you've ever read. Skyler is the perfect unlikely hero."

—John Maginnes PGA Tour player and co-host of Katrek & Maginnes on SiriusXM radio.

"The Puddle Club contains numerous life lessons for golfers of all ages. I want all of our juniors to take this journey with Skyler."

—Eric MacCluen, PGA, Director of Instruction Applecross Golf Academy

"The Puddle Club takes you on a journey that combines both golf and life. It is a great start for golfers, especially juniors, using creativity and imagination to introduce them to this great game"

— Kevin Shimomura, PGA
Director of Instruction Ko Olina Golf Academy

"A magical read that a parent and child can share. Now go out and play!!"

—John Godwin, PGA

"The Puddle Club shows how golf and life can relate in many different aspects. Life is a journey and so is golf. This book appeals to any golfer of any age or skill level."

—Rob Coyne, Golf Instructor/High School coach.

The Puddle Club

Michael McGruther
& Gregg Russell

For Reagan

This book is dedicated to anyone who knows the joy of jumping right in.

CHAPTER ONE

THE PUDDLE

SKYLER LIE IN bed staring at the ceiling. She was not looking forward to being the new kid in school tomorrow and was already filled with that nervous-belly doom and gloom. This was her third move in six years, and that certainly is a lot for a child of only nine. This time they had moved way out into the country, far from the big city and everyone they knew and loved. Skyler didn't like moving, and didn't like losing a whole bunch of friends all at once, but Mom and Dad reminded her that she would make new friends, just like last time. They said that unexpected changes were a part of life, and the faster she learned to accept it and go with the flow, the happier she would be.

None of it made any sense to Skyler no matter how much she thought it through.

Skyler slid out of bed, peeked through the shades of her window, and sighed at the sight of dark lingering clouds from last night's rainstorm. Being stuck inside always meant the same thing: another day with nothing very fun to do and nobody to play with.

Sure, the shelves were packed with board games, but after being played a gazillion times, they stopped being fun and actually made you bored instead.

Sure, the TV had unlimited reruns of all the best shows, but once you've seen them all more than thrice, they became re-re-repeats.

Skyler had recently come to the conclusion that nothing fun lasted forever, and realizing that made her feel very sad. She let out another sigh and wondered just how boring today was going to be on the boring scale. Super boring, bordering on mind-numbingly boring, was her guess.

She heard her Mom and Dad downstairs eating breakfast, and it made her feel hungry. Since it was another do-nothing day, there was no need to change out of her pajamas before going downstairs to eat. When she got to the kitchen, it was empty except for the leftover plates and a half-empty pot of coffee. She could hear them ripping apart boxes and unpacking her dad's office down at the end of the hallway.

"There's some doughnut holes for you in the cupboard," shouted her mom from another room. "Feed yourself, because I'm helping your father."

"OK," Skyler yelled back as she opened the cupboard and instantly found the box of doughnut holes. They were her favorite kind too, the small white powdered ones. She could pinch them with two fingers and pop them right in her mouth one at a time, and that is exactly what she did, until her face was covered in sugar and she needed a drink to wash down the baseball-size doughnut mound that now filled her mouth.

As she drank straight from the milk carton, she noticed something shimmering outside the kitchen window. She walked closer to the window and looked down at a huge puddle that took over a large portion of the backyard. A bit of sunlight peeked through the clouds and like a pointed beam, it hit the puddle dead in its center. The way the light touched the water was mesmerizing, and she wanted a closer look.

She put on her rain boots, wiped sugar from her lips, opened the door to the deck, and walked out. She slipped but caught her balance, then walked slowly across the wet surface. When she looked down at the backyard puddle, it looked more like a small pond. The water was perfectly still and showed a crystal-clear reflection of herself.

She looked bored and stared at her reflection for a long time, captivated by the way the puddle reflected her and the dark clouds. That's when something really strange happened—her reflection smiled and waved, even though she didn't move at all!

Skyler closed her eyes and shook her head. When she opened them again, her reflection was still smiling, but she was not. The look on her real face was confused and slightly frightened. The look on her reflected face was all smiles and happiness.

Skyler waved at her reflection, but the reflection didn't wave at the same time. It waved back a moment later.

Now Skyler started to freak out. This was the strangest puddle she had ever encountered, and the smiling, happy reflection of herself made her want to jump right in and play. But then she thought about the mess and the cleanup and how her mom and dad would not be happy if she got all muddy. Puddle play was for baby time, and she was not a baby anymore.

The reflection had a big, happy smile on its face and waved at the real Skyler one last time. Then the reflection slowly faded away until there was no reflection at all.

"Hey! Where did you go?" she yelled out, running along the railing, searching the puddle everywhere for her reflection. How could this be? How could your own reflection wave good-bye to you and then vanish? Where did the reflection go? Skyler leaned hard on the end railing, looking down, and there was only a slight cracking sound before she was falling headfirst toward the water below.

There was no time to scream as her head was about to hit the puddle. She curled up into a ball and braced—but instead of the heavy thud of hitting wet ground, she felt the sinking sensation of falling into deep water.

When she opened her eyes, she was no longer in the puddle but instead falling gently like a leaf out of a clear blue sky over a large open space with rolling hills of green grass.

"Whoa!" was all she yelled before landing gently on the supersoft ground and then tumbling a few times before coming to a stop. It felt like squishy carpet with thick padding underneath, and the hills rolled on and on as far as her eyes could see.

"Where am I?" she said out loud as she stood up and looked around, sniffing the air like a curious dog. Her house and any recognizable landmarks were nowhere to be seen. She looked down at her pajamas, and they were drying very fast, but she was not hot. The air was just right, and the sky was the perfect shade of blue. Other than being completely lost, it was a perfect day.

Skyler took a deep breath, walked toward the nearest hill and climbed to the top in order to get a better look around her. The strangest thing about this new land was how the green hills rolled on and on and then were interrupted by large flat areas of open green. There were also large pockets of thick woods scattered about. There was something so magical and peaceful about being here. She did not feel afraid. She spotted a small, lone woodshed way off in the distance, nestled on a hill among pine trees and tall grass. A plume of white smoke billowed from the chimney.

She noticed a gigantic eagle flying high in the sky towards her. She knelt down and covered her head as It soared by, casting its large shadow on the ground like an arrow. She watched as the shadow flew a few circles around her and then went in a straight line from her position to the woodshed. She took this as a sign and decided to head to the woodshed in search of help.

The ground was so squishy and springy. She skipped her way across the green, open space.

Next she had to climb up small hills and couldn't resist running down the other side. She fell once and tumbled to the bottom. It was so soft that nothing hurt, and all she did was laugh at herself. It felt good to laugh at herself, for some reason.

She then crossed over an old rickety bridge and quickly ran through a tunnel until she came out on the other side of a babbling brook. It was a strange, twisty path that led to the woodshed, which must have been much farther than it looked, because Skyler was starting to get tired out.

She decided to take a rest when she spotted a small boulder under the shade of a tree that looked just big enough for her to sit on. She plopped down there, formed pretend binoculars with her hands, and looked at the woodshed. Not much farther now.

"Hey, wanna play?" said an excited little voice from somewhere down in the tall grass behind the boulder.

It startled Skyler, and she jumped up. "Who said that?"

"It's me—Ralphie!" said the tiny voice again.

Skyler slowly peeked around to the back of the boulder. "Ralphie who?"

"I'm Ralphie -- that's who! Let's play!"

Skyler knelt there, looking down. She could not see anything except tall wavy grass.

"Don't just stand there. You gotta really dig around and find me—then we can play!"

Skyler waved her hands around in the tall grass, parting it here and there, looking for this Ralphie character she could hear but not see.

"You're getting closer. A little more to your right, or is it your left? I get confused. Lower. Lower," said Ralphie.

Skyler moved some grass and pinched a small white ball with her fingers and slowly lifted it out. She recognized what it was immediately.

"A talking golf ball?" she said.

"Mmm, mmm, mmm." Ralphie's tiny high-pitched voice was all muffled now.

"I can't hear you," said Skyler.

"Mmm, mmm, mmm," replied Ralphie.

Skyler moved the golf ball from one hand to the next, and when she did, she saw Ralphie's face for the first time: two bright happy eyes, a small cute nose, and a huge excited smile.

"You had your fingers right on my face!"

Skyler screamed and dropped Ralphie. She'd seen a lot of strange things, but a talking golf ball with attitude was not one of them—until now. She took a couple of steps back and stood there.

"Aw, c'mon…don't you wanna play?" asked Ralphie, putting on the saddest face of all time.

"I don't have time to play right now. I'm lost and have to get home."

"I know the way home," boasted Ralphie.

"You do? Tell me, please."

"All you gotta do is take me to the first tee. It's just beyond Practiceopolis."

"Practiceopolis?" inquired Skyler. "What kind of a place is that?"

Ralphie's eyes grew big. "You really are lost. You need to go see Par. He'll get you set up."

"Where's Par?" Skyler kneeled down and picked up Ralphie again. This time she gently cupped him with both hands. He's so cute. She can't help but smile at him.

"Par's everywhere and nowhere all at the same time," mused Ralphie, the tiny philosopher, eyes rolling big for dramatic effect. "But you can usually find him in the clubhouse."

"Where's that?"

"Up there on the hill. We still have time to play if you hurry!"

CHAPTER TWO
THE PUDDLE CLUB

AFTER WHAT SEEMED like forever, they finally made it to the woodshed-style clubhouse. Surprisingly it was the size of a young child's play set, and Skyler was as tall as the roof. She could see nothing but more woods and bramble all around it. It was old and damp with moss growing up the sides. There were no windows, and the only door was too small for Skyler to walk through. There was a rusty, old, antique-looking metal sign posted to the door:

THE PUDDLE CLUB—ESTABLISHED YEAR 0.

"The Puddle Club? What is this place, Ralphie?"

Skyler inspected the sign, flicking it with her finger. It was made of steel and created a stinging sensation that she didn't expect. She shook it off and backed up a step.

"First you learn how to play the game, and then you play the game!" said Ralphie.

"But I want to get home."

"Home is at the end of the game for you and me."

"What game?"

"The great game!"

"Where is it played?"

"Right through that door."

"But I won't fit."

"Find a way."

Skyler looked at the sign for a moment. What a peculiar name for a club, she thought. Established year zero? That was a real long time ago.

Fresh white smoke billowed from the tiny chimney; the smell of hot chocolate came wafting toward her. It made her hungry and reminded her of home.

With Ralphie held gently in one hand, she stepped closer to the small woodshed, knelt down, and knocked on the door. To her surprise it creaked open, and she could see a long, rounded hallway big enough for a full-grown adult. She pulled her head back and looked over the building again.

"How is this even possible?" said Skyler.

"Anything is possible but only if you take the first step," said Ralphie.

Skyler slid Ralphie down into her pajama pants pocket, and he went quiet. She got on her knees and crawled through the doorway. When she was inside, she stood up and dusted herself off. She looked back at the door quizzically. It was now just the right size for a field mouse. A strong wind slammed the tiny door shut.

She turned around and gazed down the arched hallway, nervously biting her lower lip. Her heart started racing and she got butterflies in her stomach.

"Um…Hello?" said Skyler. Her voice echoed down the hall and disappeared.

She started walking and only had to go a short distance before coming to a fork. A sign above one side said HOOK LEFT and the other said SLICE RIGHT.

A hook left sounded a lot nicer than a slice right, so she chose to go left and found herself rounding down another hall. The walls in here were adorned with framed pictures of people jumping into puddles. People of all ages and sizes from all over the world. And they all looked happy and carefree. This made Skyler feel a little more at ease.

The farther down she went, the closer to the smell of that hot chocolate she got.

The bottom opened up into a fantastically large room, more like a fancy cave, with a vaulted ceiling and a missing wall on the other side.

Skyler stood there quietly taking in the view of rolling green hills dotted with trees. She heard a loud crackle-hiss and noticed a small wood-burning stove off to the left, and on it was a tiny pot of hot chocolate about to boil over.

"Uh oh!" Skyler hurried over to the fireplace and removed the pot of hot chocolate just in time. The handle was too hot, and she dropped the pot on the floor. It crashed, clanged, and wobbled while chocolate splashed in all directions at once.

"Oh no, oh no!" was all she could say as she danced around and tried to avoid stepping in the melted cocoa. She found herself backing away from a thick, oozing river when she bumped into something fuzzy.

She turned around and saw a large, rotund, sleeping gopher that had passed out in a comfy-looking chair that faced out toward the hills. Like an old man enjoying his Sunday nap, the gopher snored loudly. It was dressed in brown knickers with a green vest and a white collared shirt with a blue puddle logo on the sleeve. Whiskered cheeks and a tiny mouth stuck out under the brown leather cap that was pulled down slightly over its eyes. A small mound of golf balls and an old, tattered set of little golf clubs were set up on a practice area a few feet away.

Skyler cleared her throat in hopes of waking up the sleeping creature. A little louder. No luck.

"Excuse me," said Skyler in her meekest voice.

Not even a whisker twitch.

"Excuse me," she said a little louder, tapping the gopher on the shoulder. When he started to move, he frightened her. He adjusted slightly and then slid down from the lounge chair in what looked like slow motion, until he was sitting in the chocolate that had pooled on the floor around him. Still groggy, he slid his hat back and looked around.

"Excuse me, Mr. Gopher…I spilled the hot chocolate," said Skyler.

The gopher hadn't noticed her standing there. When he looked up, he grabbed his hat with both hands. "A little girl!" screeched the gopher.

"Hi," said Skyler. She waved innocently with a smile on her face.

The gopher looked down at the mess and then back up at her. "I always keep a pot on in case someone drops in. I must have fallen asleep. Thank God you arrived when you did. I could have burned the whole place down again."

"Again?" asked Skyler.

"The fourth time," replied the gopher as he shuffled into a nearby broom closet and came back with a small pail and bucket that were just his size. He started to clean up the mess. Skyler tried to help him, but he shooed her away, then stopped and looked at her again with his nose twitching slightly to take in her smell.

"So tell me…what happened?" he said.

"Like you said…you must have fallen asleep, and you left the pot on a hot stove. I touched it and burned my hand and then dropped it. I'm really sorry."

The gopher looked down, then back to Skyler. "I know what happened with the chocolate. I want to know what happened with you, how you arrived here, in the Puddle Club."

"Well…um…it rained real hard all night, and the next day there was this big giant puddle in my backyard, bigger than any puddle I've ever seen before. I was trying to see my reflection, and the last thing I remember was falling in, and then somehow I fell out of the sky and landed over in those woods. The first thing I saw was your cabin, so I came here for help."

The gopher leaned on the mop handle and smiled.

"Tell me…before the rains came…were you bored much of the time? Unenthusiastic? All blah'd out about school and life?"

"Yes…how do you know that?"

The gopher pulled a small notepad from his shirt pocket and jotted down some quick notes. "I've been doing case studies of all the people who arrive here. Some conditions that bring folks in are universal, and everyone experiences them. Truly fascinating!"

He slipped the notebook back in his pocket, wiped his hands together, and slid the mop and bucket into a corner. He grabbed a small golden golf club that was leaning against the chair he had been sleeping in. He used the club like a cane, hobbled closer to Skyler, and extended his furry little hand for their first official greeting.

"My name is Parnell Knickerbocker Rittenhouse the Third—but everyone 'round here knows me as Par."

"Very nice to meet you, Mr. Par.

My name is Skyler Russell." She used three fingers and her thumb to shake his little paw.

Par grabbed two metal cups down from a nearby shelf and poured some of the remaining hot chocolate into them. He wrapped one of the cups in fabric and handed it to Skyler.

"Here. Drink up. You'll need the energy where you're going."

"Where am I going?" she asked before taking a small sip. It was the most velvety-smooth chocolaty flavor she had ever tasted, and it made her feel at ease and focused all at the same time.

"You're going on a journey." said Par.

"I am?" Skyler didn't stop drinking until it was gone.

"This tastes so good, Mr. Parnell! Like really, really, amazingly, the-best-hot-chocolate-ever good!"

"It is the official drink of the Puddle Club. It is packed with vitamins, nutrients, charity, grace, humility, a dash of luck, a pinch of grit, and all the bravery that you'll need to make it back home." He patted on the chair he had just been sleeping in. "Come. Sit down."

She sat down in the chair and took in the view of a flowing green carpet of grass that rolled on and on, and blue sky as far as the eye could see. "How long is the walk back home going to be?" she asked.

"Walking home is not permitted. Playing through is."

"Playing what?"

"Golf."

"Golf?"

"Golf. Do you know what *golf* stands for?"

"No clue."

"It stands for Game of Life First."

Skyler nodded. She didn't understand why she had to play her way home instead of just walking, or better yet being magically transported.

"Everyone who arrives at the Puddle Club is here for a reason. And all must play one round of the great game in order to get back to where they came from."

"But I don't even know how to play."

"It's quite a simple game really. Nothing to be afraid of."

Par dug a golf ball from his pocket. This one was quiet and sleepy, unlike Ralphie. Par teed it up in the grass outside the opened wall. He turned his club cane around and took his stance. After a little waggle of the tail, he took a short little swing and chipped the ball right into the cup a few yards away.

"Wow!" said Skyler.

Par turned the club upside down and used it as a cane again. "Thank you, my dear. I make that shot every time from here…but out there, where the game is truly played, it's never a sure thing and that is what scares most people away." Clouds suddenly rolled in, and the day became dreary and damp. Cold air rushed into the room. Skyler shivered. Par felt the nip in the air as well and threw some more logs on the fire.

"Come have some breakfast, and then we will get right to work."

"When do I get to play the game?"

"After you become familiar with the tools."

"So, I'll be able to get back home today? My parents must be searching everywhere for me."

"Don't you worry about them worrying about you. Time moves differently here in the puddle compared to over there in your world. A moment out there can be a lifetime in here."

Skyler walked over to a small breakfast nook at the other side of the open room and took her seat.

Hot pancakes were already waiting for them. From her vantage point she noticed a gigantic crystal palace nestled in the woods. It had to be at least ten stories tall, shaped like a larger-than-life golf ball emerging from the ground. It sparkled in the sunlight like a gem. "What's that place over there?" she asked.

Par poured an insane amount of syrup on his pancake stack and then handed the bottle to Skyler. She tried to pour some on, but only one small drip came out.

"That's Practiceopolis. We'll get to that later. First you must eat up and store some energy."

They both began to eat. Skyler was amazed at how the pancakes tasted like whatever she imagined at the moment. She thought of strawberries, and the pancakes tasted like a mouth full of strawberries. She imagined marshmallows and was now eating mallow cakes.

"These pancakes are amazing!" she blurted out.

"It's all we serve for breakfast here at the club. They're always a big hit."

Skyler watched as Par munched through his stack like a messy kid. He ripped chunks out and swirled it in syrup before chomping down. He even licked his paws between bites.

"So, how long will it take me to get back home today, in puddle time?" asked Skyler.

Par stopped chewing and gazed off in the direction of rolling hills, open fields, misty ponds, and spooky woods.

"That all depends on you. I only know one way out of here. And it's beyond those hills. There is no shortcut and no fast way to get home. You must simply play through at your own pace. One hole at a time."

Skyler looked out. It was so vast. She started to worry.

"Am I going to get stuck here forever?"

"Only if you choose to be," replied Par.

"I want to go home. Right now. That's what I want to do."

"Very well then." said Par.

Par hopped down from his seat, hobbled to a corner of the cabin and started to dig through a pile of old golf clubs with wooden heads and steel shafts. He dropped a few into a small leather golf bag and handed it to her. "Here ya go."

"What are these for?"

"They are your tools. You'll use them to play until you reach the ninth hole. That's where the only way back from the Puddle Club to your home can be found."

"But I don't even know what to do with these…things."

"Clubs."

"Clubs. I've never even held one before." Skyler pulled one out of the bag and inspected it.

"That's your eight iron." said Par.

Skyler gripped it with both hands like a baseball bat. Par gently pushed the head down toward the ground. "Like this," he said while adjusting her grip. Next he waddled around and adjusted her stance, ending with a slight push on her right shoulder so it was slightly lower than the left. He stepped back and inspected her pose. "Looks good. Looks good. Now come over here and give it a swing."

She followed him from the table to a tee box at the end of a narrow walkway that jetted out over a ravine. Skyler looked down and felt sick. She shivered as the wind blew.

"It's nippy out here, Mr. Par!"

"Don't matter. The game must be played if you want to get home. Get back into position and take a swing."

Skyler stepped across the ball and positioned herself so that she was aiming toward the distant woods. As she started her backswing, Par yelled out, "Stop!"

Skyler froze in position and looked back at Par.

"I almost forgot to tell you the three questions," said Par.

"What are they?" asked Skyler.

"The first question you must ask yourself is, where do you want the ball to go?" Par stood there and waited. "Go ahead—ask yourself."

Skyler lowered the club and asked aloud "Where do I want the ball to go?"

"Good. Now answer your own question," said Par.

"I want the ball to go…into the hole?"

"You can't answer a question with a question. Try again."

"I want the ball to go in the hole."

"Good! Next you must ask yourself what tool you'll need to make that happen."

Skyler looked at the bag of clubs and then the target. "What tool do I need to make this happen?" she said under her breath.

"The bigger the club head, the farther the ball can go," whispered Par.

Skyler looked at the club she was about to hit with and realized it was way too small for the task. The hole was far away and marked by a blue flag on a stick. She switched it for the biggest club she had—the driver. "This one should do the trick."

"And the last and most important question is this: Where should you hit the ball so that it goes where you want it to?"

Skyler looked between her club head and the sleepy-faced range ball while asking out loud. "Where should I hit the ball so that it goes where I want it to?"

The sleepy range ball yawned and then answered her with a groggy, disinterested tone. "Dead center of the club. There's a mark. Hit me with that mark and watch me go."

Skyler inspected the club head and saw a mark right where the ideal spot was to hit the ball. She then took her stance and checked her target one last time before taking a swing. In her mind the swing felt like it happened in slow motion, but in reality she cracked the club like a whip—*snap*—and the ball went soaring toward the distant flag and landed on the putting green before rolling slowly into the hole.

"Yes!" shouted Skyler.

"Great shot, kid!" yelled Par.

Skyler stood there in awe of her own shot. It was a mesmerizing moment, and it ignited a fire in her belly. "I can do this. I know I can—but first I want to hit some more balls in Practiceopolis, because that place looks totally cool."

Par nodded. "Practice is good, but remember this— you'll never find your own personal par until you are brave enough to play the game."

"My own personal Par?"

"Everyone has a different par for the course of their own life."

"OK, now I'm confused."

"Par is a system of measurement. Out on the course it's the number of hits it should take you to reach the target. In your life, personal par is the number of tries you need in order to complete any challenge."

Skyler nodded like she knew what he was talking about, but really she still kinda had no clue. How could everyone find their own Par when Par was standing right in front of her?

"Any challenge?" asked Skyler.

"Any challenge. Suppose you're not great at memorizing times tables, and you keep failing the timed tests in school. If you keep at it, develop a process, and practice religiously, eventually you will pass that test. The number of tries it took you is your par number for that particular situation."

It was starting to sink in now. Skyler remembered how it took her only two tries to ride a bike without training wheels back when she was five. It took her cousin Ella six tries. So Skyler had a par two when it came to bike riding, and Ella had a par six.

"The lower the score, the better, right, Par?"

"The lower the score, the more of a master you are at what you're doing. Better is not what matters. And anything can be mastered over time."

"This is a lot to think about," said Skyler.

"These are the rules of the game. And now it's time for you to decide where you'll begin the journey home—jump right in and play or spend a little time at Practiceopolis first?"

Par leaned on his club and twiddled his paws impatiently. Skyler nervously bit her lip as she thought about her choice. She's never even played until falling into the puddle, and now her only way home was to play through? This seemed like too much too soon.

"I'm going to Practiceopolis. It's the smart thing to do," stated Skyler.

Par exhaled deeply. He had hoped she would be the one who dared to just start playing. He swore it was the best way home.

"Well then, the choice has been made," said Par. He slid the old tattered golf bag toward her. It only contained four clubs. "You have one driver. That's for hitting the long shots. One eight iron. That's for those middle shots. One pitching wedge. You use it to get up onto the green when you're close. And lastly—one putter. This is your most important club."

Par helped Skyler slide the clubs onto her back like a backpack. He adjusted a strap, and it hung just right.

"Which way is it to Practiceopolis again?" asked Skyler.

Par lifted up his club and pointed to doors on the other side of the great room. "It's right through those doors and down the crystal hallway."

Skyler nodded and looked at the big wooden double doors with crystal golf balls as handles. Remembering Ralphie, she patted her pocket gently and started toward the doors.

"Gotta practice first, play later," she muttered to herself.

"One last word of advice...if I may," quipped Par just as she was about to pull open the doors.

"What is it?" she said.

"Respect those clubs, and they will respect you back. They are your only connection to the ball."

"I will."

Par watched as she used all of her strength to pull back the heavy double doors. She turned around and gave him one last wave good-bye as the doors slowly closed.

"Good-bye, Mr. Par! Thanks for everything!"

CHAPTER THREE

PRACTICE
MAKES PERFECT

THE MOMENT SKYLER started down the crystal hallway, she was enchanted by the sweet smells of fresh-cut grass and lemon blossoms that came wafting from the floor vents. The entire hallway was made of crystal, from floor to ceiling, and adorning the walls were pictures of Practiceopolis record holders.

Davey McGurk, fourteen, longest indoor drive two years in a row.

Chevy Carlson, nine, Putt Master Flex reigning champion.

Tiny Tina Tinkerton, eight, Hole in FUN all-time winner.

Each golfer was pictured with some cool-looking fancy golf club or new shirt he or she had won. It was exciting to imagine all the prizes one could win in Practiceopolis. Skyler started to get hopeful, because she knew that with a little practice, she could be good too and maybe even win an award before she left for home.

At the end of the hallway, a set of crystal double doors whooshed open as Skyler approached. She stood in awe of the sight of an enclosed paradise golf park made of multiple levels, with golfers hitting balls from perches that overlooked a massive central putting green. The place was buzzing with action and sounded more like a carnival arcade than a golf training area.

"Welcome to Practiceopolis!" sang the fancy-looking GreetBot 3000 as it slid right in front of Skyler's view.

The robot resembled a female golfer wearing a mini skirt, top, and a cap. Its animatic face was so real that it almost seemed human.

"My name is Welcomina, and I am here to get you set up in our beginners' training program."

"Hi, Welcomina. I'm Skyler Russell, and I'm ready to practice a little before I play the game."

"A little? How about a lot? Smart golfers practice more than they play."

"They do?"

"If you'll just follow me, I'll take you to your assigned personal instructor, and she'll bring you to the pro shop."

"What's in the pro shop?"

"Everything you'll need to be a truly great player, like a pro."

"I already have clubs and a ball. What else do I need?"

"The latest shoes. A better driver. A range finder. Special balls that can find the target even if you don't. Techniques and tips from the very best of the best golf instructors. You need what we have, and you're not leaving until you get it. Got it?"

"I guess so."

"Good!"

Hearing all of this filled Skyler with confidence. How could she fail when every tool and bit of instruction one could ever need was just waiting for her, right here, in Practiceopolis?

She happily followed Welcomina through the dome and was amazed at every sight they passed. She watched as golf cart drones zoomed around catching balls before they could land on golfers in the putting zone. She saw a boy her age working with a Range ProBot. The ProBot gave the boy candy after every good swing.

"This place is so cool!" said Skyler.

"I knew you'd like it," replied Welcomina.

Just then a new Range ProBot 9000 rolled up alongside them with its lights flashing like a police car. Range ProBots came in all temperaments, and Skyler's was one of the most intense in all of Practiceopolis.

"Skyler Russell! There you are, sweetie. I have been searching all over for you," said the Range ProBot in the voice of a charming older woman. Pictured on the bot's facial screen was the sweet look of a golfing grandma wearing a pink golf cap. ProBots all basically looked the same except for the main screen at the top, which could animate into the face of a wide variety of golf instructors. They were boxy, and each had one center wheel that seemed to defy gravity. Housed inside the body were drawers with prizes and hard-to-get tools that students could win. One drawer right in the center had a picture of Parnell on it.

Welcomina's job was done. She saluted Skyler before heading back to her post at the main entrance. "Good luck,

Skyler," she said. "I know that with a ton of practice you'll find your Par."

"Practice makes perfect," said Skyler.

"Perfect is the goal," replied Welcomina before she zoomed off.

The Range ProBot faced Skyler and looked her up and down. "Skyler, you can call me Coach Maggie Mulligan. I know all of the best drills and practice activities you can do to improve your chances of getting through the game and finding your par."

"Thanks, Maggie. I need a lot of help. Mr. Parnell just showed me the basics, and that's all I know."

"The basics get you basically nothing. Old Par doesn't do things the way we do. That's why he's mostly alone, and everyone likes being here," said Maggie. A small lift folded out on the back side of Maggie. Two grips popped out of the sides. "Hop on and hang on, Skyler."

Skyler stepped up and grabbed the grips that were golf club handles. "Where are we going?"

"To the pro shop." Without warning, Maggie started around the track that connected all of the levels. She picked up speed, and Skyler's hair was flying all over her face, but she was having a blast. Maggie sped up as she rounded the dome up to the second level. She went faster and faster, and Skyler laughed louder and louder. This was way too much fun. They passed other instructor bots and their students working on shots in one of the many practice booths. Skyler remembered that she wanted to get home, but Practiceopolis was the most fun she'd had in a long while, and she had just gotten here.

"Weeeee!" yelled Skyler as they rounded another level up.

Maggie hooked a right at the top and zoomed into a large, beautiful pro shop with a glass floor, so shoppers could see all the action below.

Skyler looked down and felt sick to her stomach.

A ProShopper AssistBot sped toward her. It had a different item in each of its six arms, and the face on its screen was a superslick salesman with a shiny, white-toothed smile.

"Hi there, junior golfer; welcome to the pro shop, where you can buy your way to the tippy tippy top. All you need is the newest and best of everything, and you'll be a champion, guaranteed. It's that simple!"

Skyler looked down again. "We're already at the tippy top."

"Not the top of Practiceopolis—the top of your game, where you find pars at every turn and make it look easy. Why? Because it is easy! All you have to do is buy all the latest gear, watch all the latest instructional videos, and always learn the newest and greatest swing adjustments—and of course practice, practice, practice all the time. Only play when you're good and ready, and you cannot lose!"

"Practice makes perfect is what my grandma always said." said Skyler.

"She is one smart lady! Perfect is the goal! Perfect stance. Perfect swing. Perfect, perfect, perfect!"

Skyler felt a sinking feeling as she realized that only perfect would do. She'd heard it all her life too. Whenever she did a good job on anything, her parents would say, "That's perfect." At school when she handed in a paper on time, the teacher's response was, "Perfect, thank you." It was now clear that perfection was the only way home, and that made Skyler truly afraid for the first time since arriving in this strange land.

"You better show me to the best stuff, because I want to be perfect too," stated Skyler.

The pro shop bot smiled with glee. "Fantastic. Let's start with some new shoes. Just swipe the screen on my chest to see all of the models."

ProShopper's belly morphed from golf shirt to a touch screen with shoes on the display. The first pair were red with black lines. "The Hawk Tail golf shoe is the industry leader in ball-to-spike positioning ratio to better enhance your swing every time—guaranteed."

Skyler swiped to the next pair. It was a rainbow-colored high top with clouds around the ankles.

"These are pretty."

"Pretty exclusive too. Only four pairs of the Cloud Bow shoe exits. They're one hundred percent guaranteed to get all of your drives sky high."

"I think I need those!"

"Lucky you. I'll put them in your basket."

"What's next?" asked Skyler, who felt like a total natural at shopping. Shopping was another cool and fun thing about Practiceopolis. It really seemed like all the action was in here and not out there where the true path home awaited.

"Next you need to pick an outfit. Practiceopolis has strict rules that golf attire must be worn at all times. Take a look at these shirts. All of them protect you from the sun, but only two have added powers."

"Show me those first."

The first shirt was bright red with white letters across

the chest that said "The Opolis" and over the words was one white arching line that made a dome.

"This shirt's special power is it entitles you to unlimited refills at the soda bar."

"How does that help my game?"

"The game makes you thirsty."

"I guess you're right. I need that."

Skyler continued to toggle through the catalogue of goodies and amassed a huge shopping basket full of items like a hat, shoes, shirt, skirt, distance reader, range finder, wind velocity meter, golf balls "guaranteed to find the hole," and something called "the gripper," which claimed to "lock" your hands into the perfect grip before each shot.

The more Skyler added to her cart, the more confident she became about how easy it was going to be to get home without even trying.

"I think that's everything I'll need," said Skyler.

"All we have to do now is fit you with better clubs, and then you can begin to practice," replied Maggie.

"I already have clubs that Parnell gave me."

"Those old things? They look like they'll fall apart with one good hit...and you're missing so many clubs. You need an Unobtanium Driver, quadruple forged irons numbers two, three, four, five, six, seven, eight, and nine, pitching wedge, sand wedge, sandwich wedge, and putter. All you have in your bag is a beat-up old driver, eight iron, pitching wedge, and this joke of a putter," said Maggie with the tone of a disapproving grandma as she picked through Skyler's clubs with disgust.

"Parnell gave me these clubs and said to respect them and they will respect me," Skyler replied.

"Parnell likes to hand out old junk clubs from a bygone era. He's trying to get rid of them, my dear."

Skyler sensed that she was being lied to. She had promised to take care of the clubs, so she was going to keep that promise. "I'll practice with the clubs Par gave me, and if I don't like them, I'll switch."

"You only get to shop one time."

"I can't come back to the pro shop?"

"We are literally and figuratively a One Stop Shop."

Skyler felt cornered. She was being forced to buy new clubs before even trying the ones Par gave her. She knew she could hit the driver well. The other clubs she had no idea about.

"Time is running out. Your lesson is about to begin."

Skyler stared at the fancy, shiny clubs on the screen. Her finger hovered over the "add to cart" button. She gulped.

"Tick tock," said Maggie.

Skyler closed her eyes and pressed the button.

"Excellent choice! You can toss those old junkers in the garbage. Your new clubs will be delivered to your lesson booth."

Maggie's chest screen switched from an overflowing shopping basket of golf gear to three numbers rotating on the screen.

"Stand by for your total bill."

"Bill? But I don't have any money."

"We don't take money here in the Practiceopolis pro shop."

Skyler watched the numbers twirl as the calculations were being worked out.

"Really? What do I pay with?"

The numbers stopped one at a time: 3...6...5...then in solid red, the number 365 flashed on her screen.

"Now I call that a bargain!" exclaimed Maggie. "You must be lucky, because all of that gear and the lessons will only cost you three hundred sixty-five days in Practiceopolis."

"But that's an entire year!"

"I know. Isn't it awesome? Just think of how good you will be by then."

"No. It's not awesome. I need to get home. I can't be stuck in here for a whole year."

Maggie frowned the most uncaring frown you can imagine. "Well, that leaves you with only one choice, and that is to leave Practiceopolis and play through without any chance of getting home."

"Why can't I just practice a little?"

"You have to take items out of your cart."

Skyler touched the screen and inspected her cart again. She started to delete items until everything was gone except for the balls that find the hole.

"Fine. I'm only getting some hole-finder golf balls. Now how much time do I get to practice?"

Maggie's number wheel started to spin again. Skyler watched with wide-eyed anticipation as it stopped at 365 again.

"What? That has to be a mistake," said Skyler.

"I'm afraid not. Those balls were on sale, because you were getting a package deal. Now they are back to the full price."

Skyler sighed, and her shoulders slumped a little. She looked outside of the dome for the first time and saw the fairway of a hole stretching off into the horizon. It looked so scary and lonesome out there, but in here felt like a lie and a trap.

"Do I have any other choices?"

"Tick tock."

"I guess I'm choosing to play through then."

The expression on Maggie's facial screen turned to shock. She looked like she was going to short circuit. A red spinning light popped out of the top of her head, and a loud siren began to wail. Everyone taking lessons stopped and looked up at the commotion. Even the ball collecting drones stopped.

"What's happening?" asked Skyler.

"Nobody leaves Practiceopolis without practicing!"

Just then the ceiling of the dome opened up, and a large flying golf cart drone descended into the pro shop.

Two small GoByeBye Bots lassoed both of Skyler's arms and dragged her onto the golf cart. Then they loaded the old leather bag of clubs into the back.

"Wait a minute! What are you doing?" she yelled out. It was all happening too fast.

Maggie looked at her, and with a phony smile said, "Good luck finding your way out there. Say hi to all the other lost souls for me." And then she let out a sinister and evil cackle.

Skyler slid down in the seat and hid from view as it lifted her up and out of the dome. As soon as the cart was clear, the dome slid shut again, the sirens turned off, light music returned, and everyone got back to practice, practice, practice, because it's the only way to reach perfection.

Chapter Four

The First Tee

The drone golf cart lowered to the ground at the first tee box. It was located just outside the Practiceopolis dome, at the end of a long ramp. She could still see and hear all the excitement going on inside and wondered if she had made the wrong decision. Bright lights flashed, and a young boy was dancing all around on the putting green. He had just won a prize for an amazing shot. Skyler got out of the cart and took her golf clubs. The cart drone lifted up and returned to the dome.

She turned around and looked down the fairway again. The trees seemed to grow taller and lean inward while the fairway stretched longer. She closed her eyes and shook her head, hoping it was just a hallucination, but when she opened them again, she realized it was not.

"Why is this happening?"

Feeling defeated before even trying, Skyler sat down at the end of the tee box and let her feet dangle over the ledge of the mound. She stared down the fairway with an angry look on her face and started to cry, knowing the road home was going to be difficult, with no guarantee she would ever make it.

The world felt heavy. She didn't have the energy or desire to begin. She sighed again, wiping the tears from her cheeks.

"Let's play!" said the muffled voice from deep inside her pajama pocket.

"Ralphie?" said Skyler as she dug him out and held him in her hands. "I forgot all about you."

"You want to get home?"

"Badly."

"So do I. Let's play!"

"But I barely even practiced, and I don't know how to play."

"All you've got to do is try."

"But what if I never find my personal par and never find my way home?"

"Eventually you will. Everyone does."

"If that's so, then how come you were lost?"

"Because I'm a golf ball. I don't think for myself. I do what you tell me to do, and that's it. The last golfer I served quit and left me there."

"Where is home for you, anyway?" asked Skyler, while tilting her head to one side and inspecting Ralphie a little more closely. Ralphie's eyes grew big and happy as he talked about home.

"When you send me into cup on the ninth hole, you don't get me back. I get to ride the undercourse highway all the way back to the Great Latheroo!"

"The Great Latheroo?"

"It's pure heaven. First I get bubble washed in hot water then scrubbed until I shine. Next comes the cold dip—I hear it's refreshing—then I get touched-up and have any marks removed from my body."

"What happens after that?" asked Skyler.

"I get put back into the distributor and wait until someone takes me out again so we can play!"

"You want to play until you get home just so you can play again?"

"After my bath."

"Why?"

"Because that's what I was made to do! Playing is the game of my life."

Skyler stared at Ralphie, thinking about what he had said. She remembered hearing adults sometimes say that life is just a game, but that never made much sense until now.

A rustling sound over in the tree line caught her attention, and she looked toward it. All she could see was the brown tail end of a gopher as it hurried back into the woods.

"Mr. Parnell?" said Skyler aloud. "Come back! I need you!"

She waited for Par to come out of the woods, but he never did.

"I guess that wasn't Par."

"It was your personal Par checking in on you. The more you understand the game, the more he appears."

"Finding my personal Par is the only way to win the game and get home, isn't it?"

"That is how it works," said Ralphie. "But there is no winning in golf just like there is no winning in life. There is only a good round or a bad round. A life well-lived or a life wasted."

"You can't win this game?"

"You can't beat golf. You can only play your best and have a good round."

"I see," said Skyler.

"Playing is the key," said Ralphie.

"The key to what?"

"Life."

Skyler stood up and held Ralphie out so he could see the fairway.

"Well then, are you ready to play?"

"Every minute of every day!"

Skyler teed up Ralphie just the way Parnell had shown her. She then got into her stance, looked down the middle of the fairway, and checked her target.

"Where do I want you to go?" asked Skyler.

"Right down the middle of the fairway," said Ralphie.

"What tool do I need to make that happen?"

"The driver!"

"How am I going to use that tool to get you there, Ralphie?"

"Hit me with the mark on the club head and watch me go, go, go!"

Getting excited about playing through for the first time, Skyler settled into position again and got comfy. One last check of the target before—*swing*—she hit Ralphie with the sweet spot of the driver and he went zooming out of the tee box.

"Weehoooo!" screamed Ralphie as he soared through the air. "Here we go!"

Ralphie was all smiles as he zoomed over the center of the fairway and landed with a big hop and then a long roll. He laughed until he rolled to a stop. "Hallelujah! It's good to be alive and back in the game!" Ralphie could see Skyler running toward him. She was excited too.

"Did you see that, Ralphie?"

"I didn't see it, but I felt it, and it felt good. You hit me just right. Let's keep going!"

"Parnell's three questions really do help," said Skyler.

With a fresh sense of excitement, Skyler fished around in her golf bag for the right club while looking at the pin and flag in the distance.

"Where do I want you to go, Ralphie?"

"Into the hole!"

"That's right."

"What tool do I need to get you there?"

"That's up to you."

"Right again."

Skyler only had four clubs, so it was an easy choice. She pulled out the eight iron and then took her stance above Ralphie. She lined up the club just right so that Ralphie was dead center again. She checked her target one last time before taking a swing.

Another beautiful shot arched up into the air, and Ralphie landed right on the green with a hop and a roll. Skyler couldn't believe it. She slid her clubs onto her back and ran to the green, clanking and banging all the way there. She stepped up onto the green and was surprised to see Ralphie sitting just a few inches from the hole.

"Wow!" she said, as she grabbed her putter and hurried over to Ralphie.

"Great shot," said Ralphie. "You're just one putt away."

Skyler hurried over to Ralphie and didn't bother to get into a proper stance. She held her putter with one hand and tapped Ralphie. He rolled right toward the hole, rolled around the rim and then popped out with a little bump of speed before he rolled all the way back down onto the sloped fairway. Skyler looked at Ralphie way down by the fringe and then back to the hole. Then Ralphie again. She was baffled.

"Slow down," said Ralphie, as Skyler walked down to him with a confused look on her face.

"I'm not running."

"You're not taking your time before each shot."

"That putt should have gone right in."

"But I didn't, did I?"

"No."

"Want to know why?"

Skyler nodded.

"Because you stopped caring about getting me in the hole."

"I just got excited because I'm doing so good. I'll slow down. I promise" And then Skyler took her time, and after three short, cautious putts, she deposited Ralphie into the cup.

When he hit the bottom, he yelled out "Yes!" at the same moment as Skyler did. Now they felt like a team, and as Skyler scooped him out of the cup, she started to wonder if getting home was going to be much easier than she had thought.

CHAPTER FIVE

BUMPY GREENS

THE 2ND HOLE awaited on the other side of a small footbridge that crossed the babbling brook. Skyler strolled over to the tee box, surprised at how much closer to the putting green it was compared to the first hole. A large sign close by marked this one a par three, which meant it should only take three hits to get Ralphie in.

Skyler teed up Ralphie, looking him in the eyes.

"This hole looks pretty easy," said Skyler.

"They all have different challenges," said Ralphie.

"And we're up for any challenge, right?"

"Yep!"

Skyler stood up and moved behind Ralphie. She looked towards the green while asking herself the three questions. She decided to use the pitching wedge since the hole was not very far away. Feeling confident and relaxed, she took a smooth swing and chipped Ralphie -- he blooped high in the air and then landed on the top edge of the green.

"Oh yeah!" shouted Skyler.

She put the club back in her bag, pulled out the putter and started walking over to the green. The closer she got the more she could see that it was covered in small bumps and was set at a pretty steep incline.

It looked impossible to get Ralphie from where he landed at the top of the green, down to the hole at the bottom. He'd have to roll through a maze of different little valleys that might easily send him all the way back to the fairway.

"Is this a joke? How am I going to get you into the hole when the green is not flat?" asked Skyler.

"One putt at a time," said Ralphie. "Come look from my angle. I see the way but I can't do it by myself."

Skyler walked around the green and up the incline so that she was standing behind Ralphie looking down.

"All I see is a bumpy green."

"It might take more than one putt to get me there but a path does exist," said Ralphie.

Skyler looked at the babbling brook and then the green. She got an idea, ran over and scooped out a handful of water and carefully went back to her position behind Ralphie. She squatted down and let the water pour down his back.

"Hey! What's going on?" giggled Ralphie.

"Finding a way," said Skyler.

"You could have warned me," said Ralphie.

They both watched as the water flowed down between the bumps twisting and turning away from the hole. Only one small bit of water flowed in the right direction.

Skyler ran back to the water. This time, by pouring it at the point where the closest drop ended, the handmade river streamed rapidly down the path and went right into the hole. She went back up and took position over Ralphie. She checked the target and made sure she was aiming at the right path. When the putter head tapped Ralphie, he rolled down the same path that the water did – but he stopped much sooner. Skyler sighed.

"That's annoying." she said.

"Putting is also about how hard or how light you hit me based on where I am on the green," added Ralphie.

Skyler stood over Ralphie again and tapped him a little harder this time. He rolled a few inches and stopped.

"Now what happened? I used more power than before and you hardly moved." said Skyler.

"That's because the ground is wet and you have to factor in all of the conditions." said Ralphie.

"Putting is not as simple as it looks," said Skyler.

"Nothing ever is," added Ralphie.

It took Skyler five more annoying putts before sinking Ralphie. She picked him out of the cup and patted gently on the top of his head.

"I need to get better at putting," said Skyler.

"I think you did a pretty good job," said Ralphie.

Another par three was next. It too had a bumpy green but no water nearby to assist. Skyler patiently worked her way through it and got Ralphie in the hole in four shots.

CHAPTER SIX
YIP YIP YO

WITH THE FIRST three holes well behind her and the dome of Practiceopolis no longer visible, Skyler rounded a corner that opened on to a beautiful fairway dotted with colorful trees that were blooming with all kinds of fruit and sweet flowers. The tee box was nestled between a banana tree and a small golden well that held a golden bucket attached to a golden rope.

"What's this for?" said Skyler as she approached the well. She set her clubs down, peered down into it, and saw pitch blackness at the bottom. She grabbed the golden rope and slowly let the bucket down into the dark. It seemed to go down much farther than should be possible, but then it stopped. After a moment, someone or something tugged the rope from down below, which was followed by a short whistle that echoed up the well. She pulled the rope and brought the bucket back up.

She pulled the bucket close, looked inside, and was surprised to see a small plate with a slice of banana bread and small glass of milk beside it. She took the plate out and realized that her sudden hunger needed to be dealt with right here, right now.

"We're having a little picnic," said Skyler as she set down the plate and milk. She then placed Ralphie on the ground beside her and began to eat.

"This bread is amazing, Ralphie. I wish you could taste it."

Ralphie's eyes looked all around and then back at Skyler.

"This is not the safest place, Skyler."

"Are you kidding? It's beautiful here. I wish you could smell all of the fruit trees like I can."

"I don't need to smell, but I can feel energy, and the energy around this hole is...not right."

Barely listening, Skyler popped the last bite of bread into her mouth and watched wide-eyed as two humming birds dove and fluttered around a giant tear-shaped purplish flower on the banana tree. She was mesmerized and even tried sipping the milk with her tongue the way the birds do.

"Are you going to play?" asked Ralphie.

Skyler looked at him, smiled, then wiped the crumbs from her pajamas and put the plate and glass back in the bucket.

"Sorry. Got distracted. Let's play."

She picked Ralphie up and moved him into the center of the tee box. She teed him up and then stood back and looked at the target down at the end of the fairway. She grabbed the driver. "Ready, Ralphie?"

"Always."

Skyler stepped into position over Ralphie and didn't even take a practice swing. She just hit him, and she hit him good. Ralphie arched big but still went far. He landed on the far left-hand side of the fairway, not far from a thick row of raspberry bushes.

As Skyler strolled over to him, gazing at all the incredibly colorful fruit trees along the way, she heard the sound of some tiny creatures laughing from inside the bush. It was very faint, almost not there. She stopped and cocked her head to listen. Nothing but silence.

She grabbed her eight iron and had to put herself between the bushes and Ralphie. She heard the weird twittering sounds again. They sounded like "yip, yip, yip" followed by a not-so-nice laugh.

"Did you hear that, Ralphie?"

"I did."

"What is it?"

"The Yips."

"Are they laughing at me?"

"You better just play through this hole quickly. The longer you linger, the more they can latch on."

Just as Ralphie said that, about a dozen teensy-tiny, little trolls parachuted down onto Skyler's shoulders. They were sharp little buggers in every way. Sharp noses, sharp eyes, sharp ears, even sharp shoes! And they had beady little eyes that were always half-closed.

The Yips formed two circles, one on each shoulder, and began to do a strange circle dance while singing, "Yip, yip, yo—yo, yip, yip!"

Skyler didn't feel them land, and their dancing and singing was almost inaudible to the human ear. However, she *felt their presence,* and it was starting to make her lose focus.

"I can't keep my eyes on you, Ralphie."

"You gotta try. You gotta focus through the noise."

"Yip, yip, yo—yo, yip yip," sang the little monsters, over and over.

Skyler waved her hand in front of her face as if there were a bug there, but there was none. She took position over Ralphie again and quickly swung the club.

Ralphie arched away to the right and landed about ten feet away.

"Ugh!" said Skyler, upset at herself. She walked over to where he had landed and couldn't see Ralphie anywhere.

"I know you're here—why can't I see you?"

She listened, but Ralphie never answered.

"Yip, yip, yo—yo, yip yip."

Skyler started to panic, looking in all directions, and when she stepped back, she saw that Ralphie had been right under her foot all of this time, buried deep down in an old divot.

"There you are! I don't know what just happened back there, but I'm getting us out of here right now!"

For a moment, Skyler's panic was refocused into determination, and she went through all three questions, selected the right club, and hit Ralphie like a line drive all the way to the edge of the green.

She slid her clubs back on and didn't even notice the small army of Yips that had attached themselves to her bag. They then leaped from the bag to her shoulders and head and all started to sing and dance again.

By the time Skyler reached Ralphie, she was totally

distracted and busy looking at clouds, birds, and a whole flock of butterflies that went fluttering by.

"Ahem," said Ralphie. "Time to focus."

"Huh? What? Oh right. Let's see…"

"Yip yip, yo—yo, yip, yip." The Yips were like rowdy sailors aboard the *SS Skyler*, and their presence prevented her from being able to think clearly about anything for too long. She had her pitching wedge in hand and looked down at Ralphie—but he looked like three Ralphies. Then he became one Ralphie again before going back to three.

"What's happening to me?" asked Skyler.

"You're distracted!" said Ralphie.

"Look at me. Look only at me."

Skyler shook her head to clear her mind and then settled her gaze on Ralphie again. He smiled at her. She smiled back. They locked eyes. The Yips were still doing their song and dance routine when something amazing happened.

The longer her eyes stayed locked with Ralphie's, the less of the Yips' presence they could both feel. She was able to completely block out their distraction, transforming their obnoxious noise into perfect silence. Checking her target, then honing-in with intent on where the ball should be hit, were the final steps in achieving true focus. Next she asked herself the three questions, slow and methodically, like reciting a prayer.

The one thing that the Yips cannot tolerate is self-control. It's like bug spray to them, and so they started to dive off her body in droves. They scattered as far from her as possible, no more singing, no more dancing—just panic and retreat.

Skyler had total control of the situation. She was one

with the club and took a beautiful swing, chipping Ralphie within two feet of the hole. It then took three putts to get him in, but she learned to overcome the Yips and their distractions and that was a lesson she would remember forever.

CHAPTER SEVEN
TERROR ON FOUR

Skyler followed the path that rounded downhill and away from the last hole. It was lined with twisty, gnarly pine trees that led to the next hole. She tossed Ralphie into the air and caught him again with one hand. He giggled every time.

"You and me – we make a good pair," said Skyler.

"We sure do."

"Wanna know what I like best about you, Ralphie?"

"My electric smile? The way I soar through the air?"

Skyler chuckled and looked at him with loving eyes.

"It's the way you keep nudging me on to try my best. It feels good to be believed in. You're a good friend Ralphie." She tossed him into the air and caught him again.

"That's what friends are for, Skyler!"

Once she turned the corner, her heart skipped a beat at the terrifying sight that lay before them.

She stood there surveying a massive sand pit that seemed alive with vibrations and deep rumbles. The putting green was like a tiny island in the distance. It looked like a speck of light green with a flag sticking out of it from here. The sun reflected off the sand and made it feel as hot as the desert. This hole required a perfect shot under extreme conditions, and very quickly her confidence from overcoming the Yips had disappeared. Ralphie could see everything from his safe place in her left front pocket, and even he trembled with fear.

"Oh no. Not the…" said Ralphie.

"Not the what?"

"Not the…Pit of Doom!"

Upon the utterance of the words "Pit of Doom," the sand belched out a deep, menacing laugh and sprang to life. A mouth formed in the sand, and two evil eyes above it. They searched for the source of that voice.

"Who called my name?" asked Doom as the face rolled closer to Skyler through the sand.

"Oh no," muttered Ralphie.

"Whoever said that sounds delicious, and I am very hungry today," said Doom as it got close enough to see Skyler and Ralphie for the first time.

"Oh, hello there, Ralphie. It looks like you still haven't made it home. That is so sad, because you'll never make it. Today I'm going to bury you so deep in my belly that no one will ever find you again." Doom let out an evil guffaw, spraying sand chunks everywhere with his mouth. Skyler held Ralphie close to her chest so he felt protected.

"You leave Ralphie alone!" shouted Skyler. "You're nothing more than a big mean bully."

Suddenly Doom's head grew and rose out of the sand, followed by a strong, warrior-like body, until a sand demon was standing there, looking down at her. With each breath sand came from its nose and pelted her on the head.

Skyler knelt down, covering herself with one hand and holding Ralphie close with the other.

"And what are you going to do about it, pip-squeak?" said Doom, towering over Skyler and casting a shadow over her entire body.

Skyler couldn't speak. She looked up at Doom with squinty eyes.

"Nobody makes it past the Pit of Doom with fear in their gut and self-doubt in their brains. All cowards stop here." Doom let out an intense menacing laugh before slowly receding back into the pit until only the evil mouth and one wicked eye was visible. "You don't look very brave to me." said Doom.

Then Doom's mouth disappeared, and the eerie silence returned. There was not even a breeze. It was like a daytime nightmare you couldn't wake up from and escape.

Skyler stood there looking at the seemingly endless sand pit and wiped her forehead. She was dripping with sweat. "There's got to be a way…" she said.

Ralphie couldn't move on his own, but it sure felt like he was shivering with fear in the palm of her hand. She turned him around so he could see it as well. "I'm not a coward, Ralphie. And neither are you."

"Do you really think you can make it to the green in one shot?" he asked.

"The only thing I know right now is that I have to try."

"Are you sure about this? If you lose me I'm gone forever and ever until the end of time," said Ralphie. He got choked up and had to fight back his emotions.

"I don't wanna be lost for all time." cried Ralphie.

"Have faith." said Skyler.

Skyler teed Ralphie up so that his eyes were pointed toward the green. She stood back and took a couple of practice swings while Ralphie kept both eyes closed and had a worried frown on his face.

"Please make the shot, please make the shot, please make the shot," he muttered.

"Please be quiet," ordered Skyler.

She stood in position over the ball and slowly lowered the club head down behind Ralphie.

"Don't forget the three questions," he whispered.

Skyler nodded and then checked her target. She silently asked herself the three questions. Ralphie closed his eyes.

Swing—whack—Skyler nailed Ralphie and he soared in a giant arch toward the tiny green island in the middle of the Pit of Doom. Skyler jumped up and down, yelling, "Go, Ralphie, go!"

Ralphie opened his eyes and could see that he was approaching the green—when suddenly a giant sand arm reached up and snatched him right out of midair.

"Not today, loser!" said the deep angry voice of Doom.

The powerful hand then squeezed into a fist and punched Ralphie deep into the sand before disappearing in a cloud of dust.

"Noooo!" shouted Skyler. "You can't do that! I made that shot, and you know it!"

Doom took the form of a large, sloppily dressed golfer with cargo pants, an untucked shirt, a crooked hat, and a cigar dangling from his mouth. He mocked Skyler as he strutted toward her. "'You can't do that. I made the shot.' Muahahaha—I just did."

"Why are you so mean?"

"Why are you so bad at golf?"

"This is my first round ever, and I need to play the game in order to get home."

"I bet you miss home."

"I do."

"I bet your mom and dad are worried sick about you."

"Will you let me pass so I can get to them?"

"Let me think about that for a second." Doom rubbed his chin, pretending to ponder the question deeply.

"The answer is…no way little lady."

"So I'm stuck here? Forever?"

Doom nodded, then pointed across the way toward what looked like frozen sand statues of golfers of all ages and sizes. "You'll be a nice addition to my collection of scaredy-cat statues."

The thought horrified Skyler. She looked at all the frozen people and the looks of fear and uncertainty on their faces, no confidence, just anxiety and sadness.

"Your shoes are ugly too," noted Doom.

Skyler looked down at her rain boots and didn't see anything wrong with them. She lifted her club up and poked at Doom. "Leave me and my shoes alone, ya big sloppy mean-o!"

When her club head poked Doom's fat, sandy belly, it went right in and made him smile and chuckle. Skyler watched as Doom quickly composed himself and regained his mean scowl. She poked him again with the club, and again he laughed and tried to hide the fact that he was super ticklish. "Are you ticklish?" she asked.

Doom began to step back away from Skyler. She could tell he was afraid of her club, so she used both hands and whacked the sand right in front of her feet with all of her might, and Doom cracked up laughing before falling back into just a mouth and eyes.

"Don't you do—" he started.

But Skyler interrupted him by whacking the sand again, this time tossing a huge cloud of it into the air. Doom roared with laughter like a kid being tickled.

Now Skyler stepped into the sand pit and dug her feet around while whacking sand here and there. "This makes you laugh? You want more, big bully?" she cried out.

The more she hit the sand, the more Doom cracked up and couldn't take a shape to scare her. Emboldened by the power of her club, she skipped around the sand, taking happy whacks that made Doom fall into a rolling laughter, which made all of the sand vibrate until, like magic, Ralphie surfaced.

"Ralphie!" said Skyler as she ran over to him. His eyes were closed, and he looked sad.

"Skyler? What happened?" he asked.

Now Skyler was kicking sand with her feet and using her club to drag long lines through it in the shape of a heart. Doom was in hysterics now. He couldn't handle all the tickling.

Skyler quickly took her stance over Ralphie, checked her target, asked the three questions, put her hands into the right "key" position, and then took a huge swing that sent Ralphie and a chunk of sand up into the air.

Ralphie landed on the green just a few inches from the hole.

Doom tried to be mad at her, but he couldn't stop laughing.

"No, no...you can't...ha-ha...you...hey!"

Skyler took a couple more shovel whacks until it looked like she was standing in a cloud of sand. "That'll teach you to pick on someone your own size!" she said before climbing onto the green and putting Ralphie in.

CHAPTER EIGHT

THE FOREST OF LOST BALLS

THE NEXT HOLE had a long and wide fairway with tall trees on both sides. Having figured out the Yips and defeating the Pit of Doom, Skyler was feeling confident again. But this new confidence was a cautious confidence that she used to keep fear from creeping in unexpectedly.

She took very little time to set up and take her first shot. She stood there and watched as Ralphie hooked to the right in a wide arc, heading straight for the trees.

"Whoa!" yelled Ralphie before he landed with a thud somewhere in the bramble.

"Whoops!" shouted Skyler. "What did I do wrong this time?"

She ran toward the tree line where Ralphie hit the ground and wasn't sure if he had bounced into the woods or not. She hoped not but couldn't tell.

"Ralphie! Ralphie!" she called.

"Over here!"

"Over where?"

"Here!"

The closer she got to his voice, the closer she got to the tree line with its spooky woods. Skyler got nervous, because she could hear distant voices in the darkness.

"Have you seen my ball?" asked a strange voice from within the forest. It frightened Skyler, because it seemed to come from right behind her but nobody was there. She looked all around, frantically searching for Ralphie.

"Where are you, Ralphie?"

"Has anyone seen my ball?" whispered the voice again. It startled Skyler, and when she stepped back, she was standing right over Ralphie.

"There you are," she said while lightly dusting away the leaves and branches from around him. "I'm so glad I found you. This place really gives me the creeps."

"Me too."

"The fairway is real close. I'll have you back up there in no time."

Ralphie half smiled in worried agreement. "I sure hope so."

"Has anyone seen my ball?" said another hidden voice deep in the shadows of the thick trees. Skyler stood over Ralphie and quickly hit him without bothering to ask the three questions—he hooked a hard right again and flew straight into the forest.

"Noooooo!" screamed Ralphie as his voice disappeared in the wind.

Skyler stood there with her mouth wide open, in shock. She didn't know what to do now. Ralphie was her only ball. The deeper she looked into the woods, the more voices she heard.

"I can't find my ball," said the voice of a concerned grandma.

"Has anyone seen my ball?" asked an old-sounding man.

"I know it's right around here somewhere," said another voice.

The woods seemed to stretch all around her until she too was lost inside.

"Has anyone seen my ball?" asked Skyler, like a zombie under a spell.

She noticed other people shuffling around, also searching for lost golf balls, before snapping out of it for a moment. "Where am I?"

"This is the forest of lost balls," said the sad voice of a lost lady. She looked bewildered. "By the way, have you seen mine anywhere?" she asked meekly.

"I'm looking for mine too," said Skyler. "Have you seen it anywhere?"

When Skyler looked around, she noticed more people closing in around her, all searching the ground, kicking through tall brush, poking leaf piles, and seemingly lost and confused. All were asking the same question out loud: "Has anyone seen my ball?"

Skyler gathered herself and watched as golfers picked through the bramble like zombies. Getting out of here quickly would be really helpful right now, or else she may end up like these poor souls—lost for all time in search of their golf balls.

She shuffled her foot around a pile of branches and

stems nearby and then asked out loud "Has anyone seen my ball?" She covered her mouth after the words came flying out all on their own.

"Oh no," she thought. "The curse is taking over my mind too." The only question her brain could muster was "Has anyone seen my ball?" and it was driving her insane. She kept turning in circles, looking for Ralphie and totally lost sight of the fairway. Her heart started to beat faster.

"Has anyone seen my ball?" she asked again with more urgency. The trees seemed to stretch out around her, and she could see lost souls scattered through the forest. Only one was a kid her age. He was a boy with fire-red hair and cheeks covered with freckles. He noticed Skyler too and started to walk toward her.

"Excuse me," he said like an old-fashioned gentleman. "Have you seen my lost golf ball anywhere?"

"I was going to ask you the same thing," said Skyler.

"What's your name?" asked the boy.

"Skyler"

"I'm Maxwell."

"What's your ball's name?"

"Ralphie—what's yours?"

"Antney. He's a real funny character too. Anyway— have you seen him, my ball Antney?"

"Not yet. Have you seen mine…anywhere?"

"I'm afraid not."

"How long have you been looking?" asked Skyler.

"It feels like I just got here, but I think's it's been a long time." He looked around and kicked up some brush nearby. "Where are you, Antney?"

"Ralphie?" called out Skyler. "No, not how long have

you been here in the Forest of Lost Balls, but here…in the Puddle Club."

"What year is it?"

"Two thousand eighteen," said Skyler.

"I got here on my birthday in nineteen sixty-eight," said Maxwell. "Maybe I should've stayed in Practiceopolis longer."

Skyler knew that 1968 was a long time ago. This made her heart sink with fear that she really could get trapped here forever chasing after something she's lost. "How did you get here?" she asked.

"Same way as you. I jumped right in."

Skyler got an idea. Her face lit up all of a sudden. "That's it! You gotta jump right in to whatever you're doing in order to get it done," she said. "Everyone looks so sad and lost in here. Let's make it into a game instead." She called out to Ralphie, "Ready or not, here I come, and I'm gonna find you!"

Skyler and Maxwell laughed as they ransacked the woods around them, flipping rocks, kicking dirt, racing to see who could be the first to find Ralphie, or any ball for that matter.

Skyler felt something under her left foot. She kicked over some brush and saw a funny-looking golf ball looking back at her. It had a thick mustache, a big round nose, and two sunken eyes with thick happy eyebrows drooping over them.

"Hey, little girl. Pick me up, and give me to Maxwell, will ya?"

"I found your ball!" yelled Skyler, excited to have actually found any ball in this mess.

"Antney?" said Maxwell.

"Maxwell!" cried Antney.

Maxwell ran over and took Antney in the cup of his hands. They were both emotional about the reunion.

"I thought I was never gonna see you again, Maxy," said Antney.

"I thought you were gone for good too," whimpered Maxwell.

"Now we can get on with the game and get the heck out of here, kiddo."

"Back to the fun!" added Maxwell.

"I guess I'm going to be here for a while," said a bewildered and sad Skyler.

Maxwell turned around and looked at her, then he looked Antney right in the eyes. "The game can wait. I need to help her."

Together they searched like it was a game and soon reached the end of the woods.

There was a fairway on both sides of the narrow collection of trees they were standing in.

"Skyler!" said Ralphie, smiling, from the nook of a tree in the center of the split.

"Ralphie! How the heck did you get all the way over there?" Skyler asked as she plucked him down and hugged him.

"You hit me here. You have more power than you realize."

Maxwell and Skyler both looked at their respective golf balls and then at each other.

"Thanks," he said.

"Thanks," she said. "I hope you make it home soon."

Maxwell smiled, looked down, and kicked the brush with his foot. "Oh, I'm taking my time. I sorta like it here, and at home...there's too much yelling and fighting all the time."

"Sorry," said Skyler. "I hope it doesn't stay that way."

"It's always a bad scene." Maxwell nodded then cheered up and shrugged his shoulders. "Well, at least now I know that the way out of a bad place is to dive right into something fun."

"So true," added Skyler. "You gotta dive right in and not worry about a thing."

"See ya," he said.

"See ya," she said, and then they went in opposite directions, back toward their respective fairways.

Skyler walked out of the woods and stopped when she was safely back on the fairway. She looked into the forest, listening for the voices but could hear them no more. She turned around and finished the hole with two chips and four putts.

CHAPTER NINE

WATER BALL

As Skyler followed the path to the next hole, a powerful wind slammed into her, blowing the clubs off her back and Ralphie right out of her hand and onto the fairway. He rolled on and on.

"Whoa!" screamed Skyler as the high-pitched scream of the wind buzzed by her ears. She scrambled to grab Ralphie, and when she picked him up, the wind whooshed by her head again and sounded like it said the word *soooooon*. Then it all calmed down, and a normal soft breeze was back.

"Now that was some crazy wind! Holy cow!"

"Good thing you're learning to speak golf ball. Gustina is watching you," said Ralphie, still shaken by the close call in the forest and now the wind.

"Who's Gustina?" asked Skyler.

"Gustina—the wind goddess of golf. She can crush anyone's dreams in an instant. She can make you cry all day. She can make you run for cover. She can make me disappear forever." Ralphie closed both of his eyes.

"I'm not afraid of the wind," proclaimed Skyler.

Ralphie opened one of his eyes and looked at her. "The better you speak golf ball, the easier it will be to navigate Gustina. I only do exactly what you tell me to do. I don't think for myself."

"If you don't think for yourself, how can you be talking to me right now?"

"I have a mind of my own, but my virtue is obedience. Strict obedience to the gospel of the golfer."

"You're not making much sense to me, Ralphie."

"Each shot you want to make is like a locked door. The way you hold your club is the key," said Ralphie.

Now it started to click in her mind in a new way. She held the driver in both hands and adjusted her grip. She said, "Driver." Next she picked up the iron and adjusted her grip again. "Eight iron." Grabbing her pitching wedge and adjusting her grip once more, she said "Pitch." Familiarizing herself with all of the keys and their corresponding locks was important to commit to memory.

"Yes!" said Ralphie. "That's it! The better you know the keys to the clubs, the better our chances are of getting past Gustina."

"Don't you worry, Ralphie. I'm gonna memorize them all."

"You'll be less likely to lose me again."

"I don't want to ever lose you, Ralphie. I'll be sad when we get you home."

"Just don't forget to say good-bye before you take the last shot."

Skyler hardly noticed the giant pond to her right as she

walked toward the tee box. This hole was flat and wide. She was still busy going over the keys, and the nearby water was so perfectly calm that it worked like a mirror. The sky and clouds and even some nearby trees all seemed to be painted right on the water.

She stepped into the tee box and set Ralphie on the tee just as some clouds moved in. She took a deep breath and stepped behind Ralphie to look at her shot.

"What is up with the weather in his place?" Skyler asked. "It changes so quick."

"Hurry up and hit me. Gustina is stirring," said Ralphie.

"OK, I'm ready," said Skyler.

Even though she was just rehearsing, she didn't take much time to set up and totally forgot to pick the right key. Failing to check her target for some reason, when Ralphie was hit he blooped in a big upward arc and plopped down right in the middle of the pond.

Skyler looked at the water and could see the ripple where Ralphie had disappeared. She was taken by surprise and had no idea a big pond was there until just now. She ran toward the pond, stopped at the water's edge, and looked down at her own reflection. She grabbed her eight iron and fished around in the water in hopes of feeling Ralphie.

"Ralphie! Ralphie!" she called out. Soon she felt something kind of heavy and slowly lifted her club out of the water. Resting on the club head was a pudgy fish with big green eyes and an even bigger mustache.

"Lost your ball, huh?" said the fish. "Sucks. I know."

"I did. Do you know whereabouts he is down there?"

The fish spit some water out of his mouth like a fountain

so that it arced and landed right behind him. "He's right down there. I saw him come in. He did not look happy."

"Poor Ralphie! Can he breathe down there?"

"Golf balls don't breathe underwater," the fish replied.

"And fish don't breathe above water, but you are."

"Touché," said the fish.

"What's your name, Mr. Fish?"

"Guillaume DeBonaventura Rojas-Sanchez McNulty the Sixteenth, but my friends call me Gill."

"Can I be your friend?"

"I love new friends. We're now friends. Yay friends!"

"Will you do me a favor—as a friend?" asked Skyler in the sweetest voice.

"Just name it!" said Gill. "I'll do anything for my friends."

"Will you get Ralphie and bring him up to me?"

"I would, but I can't. I don't have any hands, and he won't fit in my mouth."

"What am I supposed to do now? I can't finish the game without Ralphie, and I'll never see my family again." Skyler's lower lip quivered. She was growing tired and frustrated at all of the of the potential dead-end traps everywhere she seemed to go.

"You should play it," said Gill. He flipped himself backward and disappeared into the water. He swam to the middle and deepest part of the pond before sticking his head out again. "He's right here," he called out. And then Gill swam away, leaving Skyler to stare at the pond like she had at the puddle that got her here in the first place.

This was the first time she was seeing her reflection and she looked more alive and excited than before. She stood there looking down the shaft of her club as if it were point-ing at the water. She wiped away her tears and remembered something important.

"You just gotta jump right in, Skyler," she said before taking a few steps back. She gripped the eight iron tightly, ran, jumped right in, and disappeared into the water.

What happened next was the weirdest thing she'd ever experienced. As she sank slowly to the bottom, she noticed Gill and three other fish, who looked and smiled exactly like him but who had different mustaches, pulling a large lily pad down over her head with their mouths. They cre-ated a large air pocket, and it allowed her to breathe.

Her feet gently landed on the soft, mushy bottom, and she could see hundreds of golf balls laying around. All of them were calling out to her, "Pick me! Pick me!" but Skyler just ignored them and looked everywhere for Ralphie instead. She spotted him and used her club to clear the other golf balls out of the way, much to their loud disappointment.

She looked up and saw the sunlight trickling in from above. She remembered where the fairway was and adjusted her stance. Next she carefully placed her hand in the right key position and looked down at Ralphie as she got ready to swing.

Everything happened in slow motion, because she was underwater. Her backswing seemed to take forever, and she hardly noticed that all of the fish and pond creatures had gathered around to watch her. She began the downswing and stayed focused on Ralphie's hopeful face. The club left a swirling funnel of water in its wake as she connected with Ralphie right on the sweet spot—he shot up, like a torpedo, and burst through the water, where he disappeared into the glare of refracted sunlight.

Skyler was surprised by the loud applause and cheers that came from all the fish and pond creatures nearby. She took a small bow before holding her breath and pushing off from the bottom of the pond. She swam up through the water.

When she broke through to the top and climbed out, she searched everywhere for Ralphie and could not believe that he was on the green, no more than ten feet from the hole.

"We did it!" said Skyler, dripping wet, as she wrung out her shirt and grabbed her clubs.

"You did it, Skyler. You saved me. Again."

"I'll do anything for my friends," she said as she confidently grabbed her putter and then walked around the green studying the hole and Ralphie's relationship to it. "I can make this shot."

"I know you can, but will you?"

"I *will* make this shot."

"That's more like it."

The clouds were scattered, and the sky was perfectly blue again. Bird songs floated in the air. Skyler stood up and took her position over Ralphie. She cast a long shadow that lined up perfectly with the hole, and knew that keeping Ralphie within the shadow lines would almost guarantee that he would go right in.

She checked her target one last time before gently moving the putter back, and like a smooth pendulum, she moved it forward and tapped Ralphie right on the nose.

"Bonk," snickered Ralphie as he rolled down the

shadow line. Skyler watched, and it seemed like it took forever, but then—*plunk*—Ralphie plopped down into the hole.

"Yes!" yelled Skyler. She skipped over to the hole and could hear Ralphie celebrating as she approached.

"She did it. She did it. Skyler really knows how to hit it," he sang in a happy voice.

Skyler knelt down and looked at Ralphie in the hole. He smiled back at her. "You did it," he said.

"That was the hardest hole so far."

"Yeah, but you *did* it."

Skyler reached down and picked up Ralphie in her hands. She cupped him and stood up.

"Did what?"

"You played through something that looked impossible."

Skyler nodded while surveying the fairway and pond behind her. She thought about Doom and the Forest of Lost Balls. It was all starting to add up.

"If you don't play through, you can't win or lose. You just freeze," she said.

"And never forget it," added Ralphie.

"Don't you worry."

Ralphie had a huge smile on his face now. He knew Skyler was truly starting to understand the game of golf and that his chances of getting home were better than ever before.

CHAPTER TEN

PERSONAL PAR

As SKYLER STRAPPED on her clubs before heading to the next hole, she heard the sound of tiny hands clapping. It came from the edge of the woods. Skyler looked toward the tree line and saw a round and happy-looking gopher wearing the same Puddle Club shirt as Parnell.

"Congratulations, Skyler!" said the gopher as he walked out of the woods and approached her with a wound-up scroll and one new golf club.

"Par?"

"I'm not the Par you're thinking. My name is Parnell Knickerbocker Rittenhouse the Fourth. I have been assigned as your personal Par."

Parnell IV climbed up onto the green, bowed before Skyler, and unrolled the scroll. He cleared his throat and began to read aloud.

"Skyler Russell, member in good standing of the Puddle Club, who has shown determination, grit, and a true understanding of the game of golf, and therefore the game of life, has officially reached her personal par and will forever be equipped with all the tools she'll need to maintain good standing in the Puddle Club. I am pleased to present to you a medal, which shows what you have achieved."

Parnell IV then took a rope necklace off his own neck and pulled it up, revealing a small leather pouch. He fished around and pulled out a small puddle-shaped pin that was reflective like a mirror on one side.

Skyler took it in her hands and looked into it. She could see her own reflection perfectly.

"What you're looking at right now is what you've earned," said Parnell IV.

"But all I see is myself," said Skyler, confused.

"You've earned yourself, because you've learned yourself," said Parnell. "You know your weaknesses and your strengths. This is necessary to being able to play well."

Skyler smiled at her own reflection for a moment before affixing the pin to the collar of her shirt.

"And here is your new club. It is a fairway wood and can come in quite handy when you're in another tough spot."

Skyler took the shiny new club and inspected it. Her name was engraved on the handle with the phrase *Game of Life First* right below it. The club head was gold plated and shiny.

"Wow. Thanks for this awesome new club...but since I've already reached my personal par, will I really need it?" inquired Skyler.

"You're going to need it and much, much more than that."

"You mean the game doesn't get easier now?"

"I'm afraid not. It just gets more and more difficult... *but—*"

"But what?" said Skyler, interrupting.

"But if you know your personal par, you'll know how to play through any situation," said Parnell IV.

"How many more holes to go?" asked Skyler.

Just as she finished her sentence, a strong wind blew through and knocked her golf bag over.

Gray clouds started to gather in the distance. Parnell quickly tucked the leather pouch back under his shirt and bowed again.

"I, uh, better be on my way now," he said, looking up at the gathering clouds.

"Why are you leaving me?" asked Skyler, while she ran around picking up golf clubs and retuned them to the bag.

"B-b-because sh-sh-she doesn't like it when we teach mortals the secret recipe for navigating the course of life!"

Skyler had all the clubs gathered and on her back. She gripped Ralphie tightly with one hand and watched as her personal good-for-nothing Par ran away to hide in the woods.

"I ain't afraid of no wi—"

Whoosh—a strong and violent gust of wind lifted Skyler right off the ground, sending her crashing into a different nearby pond, where she landed with a big splash.

"Hey, that's not nice!" she yelled out as she swam to shore with her clubs still attached to her back and Ralphie still in hand. She climbed out and let the water pour out of her golf bag while standing there looking for the pathway to the next hole.

A small tornado of dirt and leaves blocked the path. Skyler had no choice but to walk toward it, and she was so determined now. Nothing was going to stop her.

CHAPTER ELEVEN

HOWLING HORROR

THE CLOSER SHE got to the small tornado, the louder its crunching and churning sounds became. Thick forest blocked both sides, and the only way to the next hole was through the swirling mess. She took out her new fairway driver and held it like a sword as she approached.

"I'm not afraid of you! Nothing will keep me from getting Ralphie home, and I will never give up!" she called.

Skyler hacked and swung with her eyes closed as she slowly stepped right into it. The howling wind swirled around her entire body. Leaves and bits of branches smacked up against her. She opened her eyes slightly and could see the other side where the next tee box awaited.

"Why is she doing this to me?"

"She does this to everyone. It's a test!"

"A test of what?"

"A test of your desire to play the game."

"But I have no choice."

"You do have a choice, Skyler. You can choose to play just to exist or you can play with a purpose."

She was right in the middle of the tornado now. It was almost impossible to see out. What Ralphie just said stuck in her brain. She didn't realize that the choice was so obvious yet so confusing all at the same time. Either play just to get by or play with a purpose. She knew exactly what that purpose was—to get her and Ralphie home—and home was where Skyler really wanted to be.

She finally broke through and emerged out the other side. She spotted the tee box at the top of a long set of steps made from old mangled golf clubs. The railing was also made of bent and dinged-up clubs. As she climbed up, she could hear the unnatural cry of wind howling and screaming at bizarre pitches. It sounded like a lonely cat's howl followed by a hissing whisper. It sure didn't suggest fun.

Skyler reached the top and looked out at the fairway located clear across a deep chasm. The wind whipped through the chasm, whistling around rocks and pushing through holes to make those creepy sounds. The wind made Skyler's eyes tear up badly. She kept wiping them and looking at the green. It was hard to believe what was happening out there.

Six small tornados churned on the front half of the fairway. They were circling one another slowly and then switching pattern to a sort of crisscross dance. The high-pitched scream was coming from them. Skyler felt dizzy just watching. She pulled out Ralphie and faced him out so he could see what awaited.

Ralphie's eyes grew wide. He had no way to understand

what he was seeing either. "I gotta tell you a secret, Skyler," he said.

"What?"

"I've never been this far before."

"You mean you've never been home?"

"Only one time, when I was first created. Ever since then I've been out here in the game—lost, waiting, and praying to get back one day."

"We're almost there, Ralphie. You and I both are going home. I promise."

She looked from one small tornado to the next until she noticed the distinct pattern in which they were moving. Once she honed in on the pattern, she knelt down near some exposed dirt and used her finger to draw imaginary lines from one tornado to the next, like an invisible thread spun from spool to spool. She played it over in her head while looking at the dirt diagram to make sure the calculations were just right. She looked at Ralphie and said, "We gotta play through, so we're playing through. I think I see the way."

Skyler felt confident that she knew the pattern. She teed Ralphie up, asking herself the three questions at the same time. She had to move quickly, because she wanted to hit the ball at just the right moment in order to take advantage of the direction the tornados were blowing.

"Ready, Ralphie?" said Skyler.

"Always ready!" said Ralphie.

"Three, two, *one*." Skyler swung the club back, smooth and wide, and gave it a whack with more power than she ever used before.

"Gooood hiiit," yelled Ralphie as he zoomed like a

rocket over the whistling ravine and toward the first tornado. The closer he got, the more it looked like he was heading toward the stormy eye of Jupiter. He hit the first spinning cloud and instantly lost all sense of direction. He was being spun in circles so fast that he had to close his eyes.

Skyler watched from her vantage point up on the tee box platform. She was delighted to see Ralphie ping-pong-ing from tornado to tornado as if they were playing a game of keep away. He kept zipping and flipping and rolling between them until he finally shot out the far end and went blasting straight down the fairway.

"It worked!" Skyler shouted as she saw Ralphie emerge and land with a lot of momentum. He started to roll down the fairway.

"Keep going…keep going," said Skyler. But Ralphie did not keep going. Instead he slowed and then reversed until he was rolling back toward the tornados with a lot of speed.

"No way," said Skyler.

Skyler hustled down the crooked and unbalanced stairs until she was close enough to jump down to the ground. She ran across the wobbly bridge that crossed the ravine onto the fairway where Ralphie came to a stop not far from edge of the ravine. The tornados suddenly disappeared too. What kind of a cruel joke was this?

Skyler ran over to Ralphie and sat down beside him. She looked confused and almost defeated. Ralphie smiled up at her.

"Gustina is not going to let us through!" said Skyler.

"Her game is to prevent anyone from making it home," said Ralphie.

"Why does she want to keep everyone here?"

"Nobody knows for sure. All the other golf balls say it's because she'll be lonely and have no one to push around."

Now the wind was blowing at a steady rate around them. It was impossible to escape and made the simple task of standing feel like hard work.

"This hole is a par five, but my personal par is more like a fifteen on this one," stated Skyler, thinking out loud as she looked at Ralphie and then down the fairway.

The wind was so steady now that all of the trees and grass bent in one direction—toward her. Skyler took a deep breath and exhaled.

"When you're in the game and things start to look impossible...you gotta jump right in and play through."

She took her stance over Ralphie and checked her grip on the club. The wind intensified, and she had to keep all of her muscles tense just to stand straight.

"Today we play with a purpose!" she yelled.

Whack! She connected with Ralphie and sent him soaring down the fairway, cutting the wind and keeping his trajectory until a gust made him shoot up and then loop right back toward Skyler. She became angry as Ralphie came rolling back toward her with a lot of speed. He stopped a few feet from where she was standing. Again.

"I don't like you, Gustina! You don't play fair!" said Skyler.

"Life's not fair," bellowed back a deep and wispy voice from all around her.

"I don't care if it takes me one thousand hits to get there! I will never give up!" shouted Skyler.

"You're learning," bellowed Gustina. And then all of a sudden, Gustina disappeared, and the eerie calm returned.

Skyler knelt down and whispered to Ralphie. "I think she's gone. This is a par five, so if I can get you a pitch and a putt away, I can get us out of here."

"Stop talking; start golfing," said Ralphie with a sense of urgency in his voice.

Skyler stood up and took position over him again. She lowered the club and then remembered something important. She stepped back and knelt down.

"What are you doing? Hit me! Hit me!" cried Ralphie.

"We have to say good-bye first, remember?" said Skyler.

Ralphie smiled big. He really loved this golfer and was going to miss being on the journey with her.

"Good-bye, Skyler."

"Good-bye, Ralphie."

"I'm gonna miss you."

"I'm gonna miss you too."

"Thanks for finding me."

"Thanks for guiding me."

"I'm gonna tell all the other golf balls about you when I get home."

"Not me. I'm keeping everything that happened here in the Puddle Club a secret."

"How come?"

"Nobody would believe me if I tell them."

"Some will. Those will be people who have also been to the Puddle Club."

"Not everyone jumps in?"

"Sadly…no. Now hurry up, focus…and send me home!"

"Right," said Skyler as she did exactly that and got

into position, but instead of facing the hole, she faced the tee box.

"What are you doing?" pleaded Ralphie.

"Hush."

The moment she started her back swing, old Gustina blew toward her to throw her off balance. Skyler quickly jumped and twisted around so that she was facing the hole, and then she powered through the rest of her swing and connected hard with Ralphie. He leaped right off the club and rode the wind down the fairway.

Gustina didn't realize what had happened until Ralphie was quite far.

She settled all winds, and Ralphie dropped like a dead weight in the middle the fairway. He laughed hysterically. He knew what Skyler had done.

Skyler cheered and ran toward him. As she did, the wind picked up with a fury of power and knocked her sideways. She fell down and had to crawl slowly toward Ralphie, who was only held still by the chunked out divot he had landed in.

"That was well played, Skyler," said Ralphie.

Skyler fought the wind and stood over Ralphie. All of her clothing flapped uncontrollably, and her eyes teared up so she could barely even see. She held her grip and checked her target but had to keep wiping her eyes.

"This is so frustrating!" she yelled out.

"Don't give up, Skyler. You can do it. Use all of your senses." yelled Ralphie.

Skyler looked up and wiped the tears from her eyes again. When she opened them, she saw something amazing: visible lines, like transparent thin spaghetti, whipped and dipped all around her and flowed toward the target. She looked at the lines and followed one. It went past her at eye level and then lifted up and to the right, before ending somewhere up high. She found another string, and it too had a similar path, but instead of ending up on the right, it ended up on the left.

"I can see the wind, Ralphie. I see every wavy noodle of it flowing all around me." The more she dried her eyes, the less of the strings she could see. So she let them fill with water again, and her ability to see Gustina at work returned.

"When my eyes get just right, I'm sending you to the green!"

"Let's do this!" he yelled back.

Skyler took position over Ralphie and made sure she had the right grip for the club. She used her new fairway driver, and it felt truly perfect in her hands at this moment. Her eyes filled up again to the point where she could see the patterns of the wind. She looked down at Ralphie and smiled. One of her wind tears fell and landed on his nose. He giggled.

"I really have fun with you, Skyler Russell."

"I really have fun with you too, Ralphie."

Skyler checked the target one last time and then focused on the passing wind noodles. She spotted the one she wanted to hit into and used all of her might to swing back against the wind. She let Gustina do the rest of the work and simply guided her hands as the club head snapped down and drilled Ralphie right in the kisser. He zoomed into a wind noodle and shot straight toward the green with amazing speed and accuracy.

"Weeeehoooo!" shouted Ralphie as he rode the *Gustina*

Express. Next the noodle shot up so that Ralphie looked like he was a rocket being launched from the ground.

Skyler looked on. She didn't notice the last lift up.

"Oh no…" said Skyler.

That's when a dark shadow passed directly over her, and for a moment it seemed like nighttime.

Chapter Twelve

Mighty Eagle

THE MIGHTY EAGLE soared over Skyler, cutting through all of the wind noodles with his powerful, razor-sharp beak. The eagle caught Ralphie with one claw, and when he passed over the hole, he dropped him.

Skyler watched Ralphie fall, and it seemed to happen in slow motion. She could see his big smiling face and big happy eyes as he made the final step in his long journey. Ralphie fell directly into the hole.

She could not believe her own eyes. Did the eagle really just send Ralphie home? Now real tears started to run down her cheeks. Skyler walked onto the green from the fringe and looked down into the cup. "Oh, Ralphie. I'm really gonna miss you," she said.

She looked into the cup for a long while and then noticed a large shadow appear from the other side of the green. She looked up and saw the mighty eagle standing directly across from her. He was majestic and powerful. His feathers were golden and white. His eyes were piercing blue.

"Congratulations, Skyler Russell. You have played very well and with a good purpose in the Puddle Club."

"Do I get to go home now?"

"Yes. And I am your ride."

"What's your name, Mr. Eagle?"

"Mighty B. Eagle. You can just call me Mighty."

"Why did you help me?"

"I didn't help you. You did that all by yourself. And you played smart."

"I did?"

"You beat her by figuring out how to use her own power against her. I was very impressed."

"Yeah, but then you grabbed Ralphie and dropped him in the hole. I saw you with my own eyes."

"This hole is a par five. You made it in four. Factor in your personal par and it's an eagle."

Skyler looked at Mighty with a confused expression on her face.

"What's an eagle in golf?" asked Skyler.

"Two shots under par," said Mighty.

"In the Puddle Club, when you get an eagle, you literally get an eagle," said Mighty.

"But my personal par is so much bigger than…getting a you. I just got lucky."

"You know what the funny thing about being lucky is?" asked Mighty.

"What?"

"It always seems to happen to those who play with a purpose."

"Is that what I did?" asked Skyler.

"It's what you were born to do," said Mighty. "Now if

you'll please leave the clubs and the bag right where they are and come hop on. It's time for me to take you back home."

Skyler left the clubs where they were. Her mind raced with questions all of a sudden. It's what I was born to do? she thought as she looked back on the fairway and into the sprawling, sometimes gnarly, but mostly beautiful golf course she had just played on. She still wasn't even certain if this was a dream or not.

Mighty knelt down and lowered his head as Skyler approached. She saw a small saddle in the center of his back and straps hanging from both sides for her feet.

"Climb right up and get comfy," said Mighty.

Chapter Thirteen
No Place like Home

Once Skyler was securely in her seat and with both feet in the stirrups, Mighty leaped into the air and took off with a few powerful strokes of his wings.

Skyler clung to Mighty's neck with both hands.

"Loosen up…you're strangling me," said Mighty.

"Sorry," she replied.

He stopped climbing and straightened out to a slow soar. Now they could see the entire golf course below—the pond, the Forest of Lost Balls, Parnell's clubhouse.

She saw Parnell standing outside, waving up at her. Mighty swooped gently down so he could pass right by.

"Congratulations, Skyler!" said Parnell. "I knew you would make it!"

"Thank you, Mr. Parnell! I couldn't have done it without you!"

Now Mighty climbed up again, but Skyler knew what to expect and was much more relaxed about it. She saw the Pit of Doom off to her right. The big, fat, sloppy golfer monster emerged from the sand and waved good-bye to her as well."

"You're a clever girl!" said Doom. "Nobody can frighten you!"

"Good-bye, Mr. Doom! Try being nice one time!"

Mighty swooped low to the ground as they passed the large pond where Ralphie went in. She saw fish leaping out of the water like synchronized swimmers.

Whey they passed over she could see that the lily pads had been arranged to spell out *jump right in.*

Skyler smiled big, looked straight ahead and saw the rocky area where she found Ralphie. They were getting very close to exactly where she began this unbelievable adventure.

"How are you getting me out of here?" asked Skyler.

"It's a bit tricky, but I know you'll be able to pull it off. Do you see that puddle up there?"

Skyler looked straight ahead but only saw golf course and rolling hills of green. "I don't see a puddle anywhere."

Mighty banked left so that they were flying almost sideways. "Look up," he said.

Shimmering in the sky like a thin silver blanket flapping in the wind was a puddle, and through the shimmering water, Skyler could see her backyard and back porch. It looked like a painting mixed with a dream.

"That's my house! It's up in the sky?"

Mighty straightened out again and started to soar in wide circles just outside the perimeter of the sky puddle.

"It's your doorway. When you're ready I'm going to fly up as close as I can, and you have to stand on my back and leap up into the puddle," said Mighty.

"Whaaaat?" said Skyler. "I can't stand on your back while you're flying! And what if I jump and miss?"

"Have faith that I'll catch you."

Skyler looked at the shimmering scene of her backyard through the puddle-space-time continuum. She really missed her mom and dad and mostly wanted to have fun with them.

"Do you have any questions before you go?" asked Mighty.

"Yes. What did you mean by 'I was born to do this'?"

"You were born to play the game of life—to participate in the mystery with faith and purpose until you return home."

Skyler thought about this as Mighty soared gently in wide circles. She sensed that he was really talking about the world she was returning to and not just the Puddle Club.

"I'm ready to go home, Mighty," said Skyler.

"You got it, Captain. I'm circling in. Tell me when you're in jumping position."

Skyler was shaking at the knees as she carefully climbed out of the saddle and straddled it long-ways so she looked like she was surfing on Mighty's back. She wobbled and worked to keep her balance as he soared gently up toward the puddle, closer and closer.

"Almost there, Skyler."

"I'm ready."

"A couple more seconds, now…"

"I see it."

"What's the number-one rule of the Puddle Club?" asked Mighty.

"You gotta jump right in!" shouted Skyler as she crouched down and leaped with all of her might straight into the sky, penetrating the puddle vortex like a diver into the ocean. A large ripple ran across the sky as she was swallowed by the puddle, which then disappeared with a thunderous collapse.

All Skyler could see was the hazy, watery image of her backyard. She moved toward it in slow motion and then—*splash*—popped out as if she had been playing a jumping game all this time. Skyler landed on solid ground and let out the happiest cheer ever.

"This is so much fun! Wee! I love puddles!" She hopped and splashed all around until her pajamas were soaking wet. She was so happy to be home and let herself fall back so that she was laying on the damp grass with her boot heels still in the water. She gazed up at the clearing clouds with blue sky showing through and smiled.

Skyler was genuinely looking forward to school tomorrow and all the challenges the new year would bring. Having a strong faith in her ability to play the game created a newfound and everlasting self-confidence. Knowing how to measure personal par in any situation made her revel in the fact that she could master anything that her mind was set to.

She looked up and noticed her parents watching from the kitchen windows. She waved them down and started to skip and splash again.

A few moments later both Mom and Dad came out onto the deck and then down the stairs. Without saying a word, they too began to jump and splash in the puddle until everyone was a mess and laughing. It was a good day, a very good day.

The End

GOLF BALL HEAVEN

THE LAST THING Ralphie remembered was falling into the ninth hole. The bottom fell out, and he dropped for what seemed like forever until he plopped down in a lazy river. The lazy river was warm and soapy, and there was even calming music piped in.

A small, cute robot swam over to Ralphie and immediately started to clean off all of his blemishes. Its many robot arms were able to polish, shine, and rotate Ralphie with great efficiency.

"Where am I?" asked Ralphie.

"You're home. Please relax and watch the highlight reels from your epic journey," said the bot.

Ralphie rotated around so he could see highlights from his game with Skyler being broadcast on screens that lined the spa zone. The moment Skyler first picked him up brought a tear to his eye. Their encounter with the Pit of Doom was frightening to relive. Being played from the depths of the pond was truly something special but paled in comparison to the physics and math it took for Skyler to beat Gustina.

When Ralphie reached the end of the lazy river, he was shiny and new, and he sparkled like a diamond. He rolled out through a one-way door and was carried away on a feather-bed conveyor belt with a line of other golf balls, like chicken eggs in a factory. They basked under a warm light and were all headed toward a black hole at the end of the tunnel. One by one the balls dropped off the end and disappeared.

When Ralphie went over the edge, he didn't have far to fall. He landed on a pile of other clean and spiffy golf balls, all cramped together in a stuffy, hot box. There was a lot of chatter as the balls shared stories of their journeys home with one another.

"Hiya. Anyone know how long we stay here?" asked Ralphie.

"Until we're needed, son. Until we're needed."